KING COO
A genius!
(possibly bonkers?)
Coo
COO'S CROWN
EVERY KING has one
COO'S SPEAR *
For fishing, Poking things (mostly baddies) and toasting marshmallows.
(* includes firefly lantern)
BAG
full of PLANS, gadgets and SECRETS.
(and wombat snacks)
a BEARD!
(yup! That's right! Is it real? who knows? It's a cracker though, isn't it?)

Ben Pole
cornflakes
clever in the noggin
On the lookout for bullies
BAG (I don't KNOW WHAT'S in here)
SKinny as a bean Pole
more cornflakes
sneakers, for ...um, well, sneaking
BEN as '3rd Tree' in School Play: In his Pants and painted green
HA HA!
Ben = VERY good at hiding
*
CAN YOU SPOT HIM:
at home?
at School?
No? See, I told you he is good at HIDING!

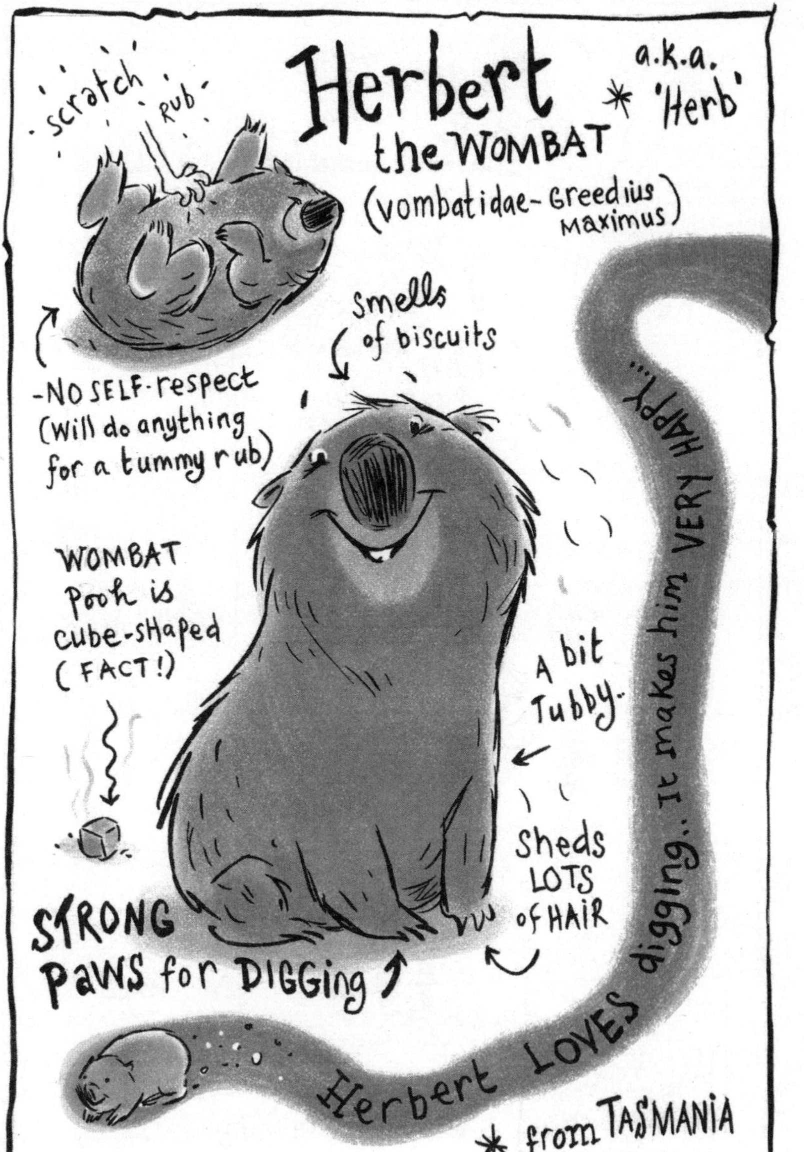
Herbert
the WOMBAT
a.k.a. * 'Herb'
(vombatidae-Greedius Maximus)
scratch
RUB
-NO SELF-respect (Will do anything for a tummy rub)
smells of biscuits
WOMBAT Pooh is cube-sHaped (FACT!)
A bit Tubby..
Sheds LOTS of HAIR
STRONG PaWS for DIGGing
Herbert LOVES digging.. It makes him VERY HAPPY...
* from TASMANIA

Also by Adam Stower:

King Coo

King Coo: The Curse of the Mummy's Gold

King Coo: The Thing from Space
is a
DAVID FICKLING BOOK

First published in Great Britain in 2020 by
David Fickling Books,
31 Beaumont Street,
Oxford, OX1 2NP

Text and illustrations © Adam Stower, 2020

978-1-78845-070-6

1 3 5 7 9 10 8 6 4 2

DAVID FICKLING BOOKS Reg. No. 8340307

A CIP catalogue record for this book is available from the British Library.
Typeset in 12.5/19pt Goudy Old Style by Falcon Oast Graphic Art Ltd.
Printed and bound in Great Britain by Clays, Ltd, Elcograf S.p.A

For my Mum and Dad who are amazing,
~with love.

11:18 pm

The tall thin figure stood pressed against the window and strained to see clearly through the dark wintry night.

There it was again! High up in the sky! A green light, glowing brightly and then dropping slowly, straight down, getting lower and lower until it vanished from sight.

The figure dashed to a desk, snatched up the telephone and dialled quickly.

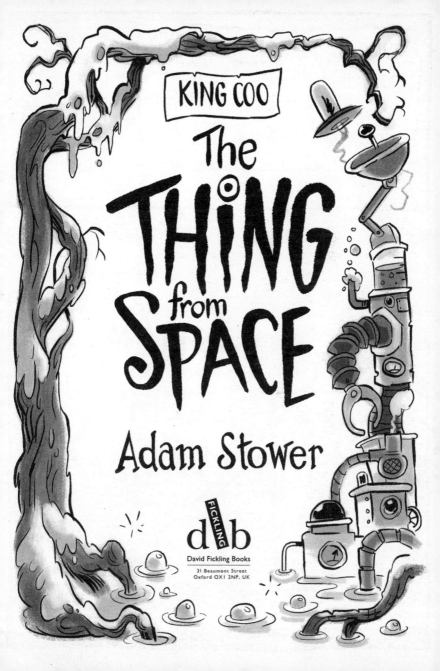

KING COO

The
THiNG
from
SPACE

Adam Stower

db FICKLING

David Fickling Books

31 Beaumont Street
Oxford OX1 2NP, UK

CHAPTER ONE

B en pressed the button.

With a soft FWUMP, a flare shot up high over their heads, burning bright pink against the winter sky.

'Not bad, eh?' said Coo. 'Now try that lever.'

Ben grabbed it and pulled. He felt the deck shudder as beneath him pulleys whirred and switches clicked.

'BOMBS AWAY!' yelled Coo over the roar of the wind. She and Ben leaned over the side to watch several bundles drop through the swirling snow and burst apart, showering the ground far below with hundreds of acorns, seeds and conkers.

'Ha! Brilliant!' said Ben. 'What else can it do?'

'Oh, loads.' Coo grinned, her long beard whip-cracking in the breeze.

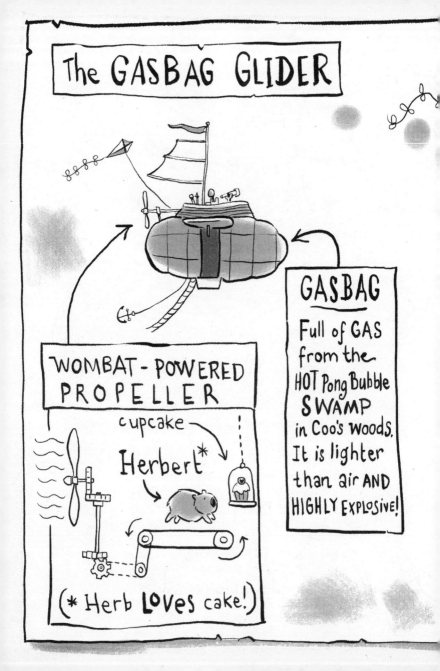

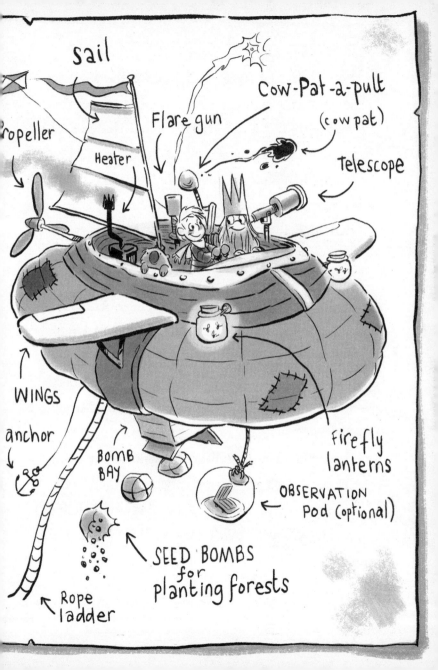

Ben took the wheel and steered the Gasbag Glider into the wind. As he cast an eye over the many knobs and levers that cluttered the control panel he let out a squeak of excitement. It was just SO brilliant! This was without doubt Coo's best Coo-traption ever!

Ben looked at her and smiled. Not everyone had a best friend like Coo. True, she might stand out in a crowd, what with her crown, spear, pet wombat and her long flowing beard. And yes, she had a nasty habit of testing out her genius inventions on him when he least expected it, but Ben wouldn't have it any other way. He grinned. Who else got to fly to school in a home-made Zeppelin?

Ben tipped the wheel forward and whooped as the glider dipped and swooped between the clouds.

He had just skimmed a particularly huge fluffy grey one when a foul pong suddenly filled his nostrils.

Ben winced. It smelled horrible and it was so strong it made his eyes water.

He turned to Coo and caught her wrinkling her nose and casting a sidelong glance in his direction.

'It's not ME!' protested Ben, pinching his nostrils shut. The smell thickened.

They both turned to look at Herbert.

'No, hang on!' Coo frowned, tapping a dial with her knuckle. 'It's not Herb. We're losing altitude.'

She peered over the side and squinted at the gasbag. 'I thought so. We've sprung a leak.'

'Wait! What?'

'That's what that whiff is. It's the Hot Pong Bubble gas. It's a tad explosive.'

'Don't PANIC? This is the perfect time to panic!' Ben gripped the side and peered at the ground. It was definitely getting closer. 'Either we're going to crash and then explode, or explode and THEN crash!'

'You don't half fuss, Ben,' said Coo as she slipped some straps around him. 'We'll probably be fine.'

'Probably? PROBABLY? That's really not helping, Coo, if I'm honest.' Coo handed Ben his school bag. 'Wait, w-what are you doing?' he asked, tugging at the harness Coo had strapped to him. 'What's this?'

'We need to lose some weight to gain height,' said Coo, who was infuriatingly calm, 'and there's no time like the present.'

'For what?' said Ben, backing away.

'For testing the emergency escape system.' Coo winked, and then she shoved him overboard.

'HIT THE RED BUTTON AS YOU GET TO THE GROUND,' she shouted after Ben as he tumbled through the freezing air.

He had just enough time to scream and madly flap his arms about before the ground rushed up to meet him. He fumbled for the button but missed it altogether and shut his eyes tight, expecting to end his short life as a jammy splotch.

Then, just centimetres from the ground, he slowed to a stop before being yanked back up into the sky.

It appeared that the harness Coo had strapped him into was attached to the end of a long rubber rope. Before Ben knew what was happening he burst through some thick cloud and there was Coo, at the wheel of the Gasbag Glider with Herb beside her, his tongue flapping in the breeze.

'Stop mucking about, Pole!' she yelled. 'Hit the RED BUTTON!'

'Wha—?' was all Ben could manage before he dropped back down through the cloud.

He plummeted towards a line of orange lights that twinkled below him. He was all set to hit the release button as the rope reached its full stretch when—

Ben touched down in the middle of the street. Lights flashed, engines roared and brakes squealed as cars swerved, missing him by a whisker before he shot back up into the clouds, his heart thumping against his ribs.

'It's the round RED thing!' shouted Coo as Ben rose momentarily into view from the thick clouds. 'On your harness! Just bash it!'

Ben managed to give Coo a wobbly thumbs up as he reached his peak, rather elegantly turned a full slow somersault, and dropped away again.

Every time he touched the ground he hammered at the red button, only nothing happened – it was frozen solid!

And each bounce dragged the Gasbag Glider lower and lower until soon it was skimming the chimney pots. Coo gripped the wheel and expertly steered the glider as it dipped and swooped between the rooftops with Ben dangling all the while on the end of the rubber rope.

With giant leaps he hopped and skipped through back yards and over buildings until all of a sudden he saw his school ahead.

'We're coming in fast, Ben! You've only got one shot at this now!' shouted Coo from above.

Coo lined up the glider perfectly, and with one last bounce Ben leaped over the school railings, only narrowly missing the iron spikes. He rubbed the button furiously to try to warm it up, and the instant his feet touched the ground, whacked it as hard as he could.

With a loud *ping* the harness sprung open and whizzed back up to the glider, leaving Ben safely in the middle of the snowy playground.

He watched as the Gasbag Glider rose gracefully into the sky.

'It works, then!' shouted Coo, grinning. 'The ELASTIC BOUNCE-TASTIC! Worked like a dream!'

'Like a nightmare more like.' Ben chuckled weakly, panting to catch his breath. 'See you later then, at mine?'

'We'll be there.' Coo waved, and as the airship vanished from sight in the white clouds, Ben turned and trotted through the snow to assembly.

He was late.

CHAPTER TWO

Ben managed to slip in at the back of assembly unnoticed.

He sat quietly while the headmaster, Mr Gigglethwick, was making his daily announcements, and enjoyed a moment catching his breath after his rather eventful journey to school.

He was just thinking that if he was going to survive whatever Coo had in store for him next, it might be worth spending some of his pocket money on a good sturdy helmet, and perhaps even some body armour, when—

Spl-otch!

Dotty Wiggins, sitting three rows in front of Ben, shrieked and turned round in her seat.

Oi! Who did that?

She glared through her enormous glasses, and wiped at her head with her sleeve. 'It's NOT funny!' she growled, staring at the children behind her, who all sat shrugging in their seats.

The headmaster paused for a moment, looking up over the top of his glasses, and then continued . . .

Splatch!

'EEK!' This time it was Jamal Haddad, a tall boy three seats along from Ben who groaned as he wiped his head and flicked wet gunk from the tips of his fingers. Children were starting to fidget now, nervously looking this way and that.

'What's going on back there?' Mr Gigglethwick had stopped what he was saying and stood on tiptoe, craning his neck to see what the disturbance was.

Ben scanned the crowd but saw nothing. *That means it must be coming from . . .* He tilted his head up at the ceiling and . . .

SPLOTCH!

He was hit smack in the face by a big glob of slime!

'BLARGH!' Ben gurgled, as the goo slid down his face and dribbled from the tip of his nose.

He wiped his eyes and looked up. The ceiling was dotted with dangling blobs of quivering slime! Ben frowned and held up his sticky fingers but just as he was about to take a closer look . . .

'But—'

'No "buts", Pole, I've got my eye on you!' said the headmaster, frowning at Ben across the hall. 'You children really must take things more seriously!'

The kids settled into a hush, broken only by Dotty Wiggins who said in a loud whisper, 'Well, he's got a nerve, telling US to be more serious! I mean, just LOOK at those SOCKS!'

Ben leaned to one side to see what Dotty was talking about. She wasn't joking. The headmaster's socks were lime green and dotted all over with bright pink love hearts.

They were certainly zany, and not the kind of socks you'd expect Mr Gigglethwick to choose, but that wasn't what caught Ben's attention. It was something else. Something weird.

And assembly was just the beginning. Ben's day got weirder and weirder.

My WEIRD day!

B. Pole

9.00 a.m. → Attack of the SLIME BLOBS!
I got gunked in the face by weird gloop!
I took a sample for testing.

SLIME → old yoghurt pot

9.03 a.m. → The MYSTERY of the
VANISHING shoes!! What has
happened to Mr Gigglethwick's
shoes?? I must investigate!

Gone! →

10.10 a.m. I tested the SLIME BLOB.
It is NOT alien GOO! It is rhubarb
JELLY! But why was it on the
ceiling? VERY strange...

11.17 a.m. → The AMAZING melt-proof SNOWBALLS!

Barney Bagshot got rich by selling MAGIC melt-proof snowballs for the break time snowball fight. What is his secret?

12.15 p.m. → They are BAKING POTATOES

painted WHITE! I know this beause one smashed through the maths room window and landed on my desk!

Big spud →

(Barney is in detention)

12.48 p.m. → The Case of the CREATURE SOUP!

Lunch time — Suzy Smithers started screaming that there was a CREATURE in her soup. She attacked it with a fork and threw it in the bin and was then sick all over Peggy Simms!

GRAAH!

Of the many strange things that had happened that day, Ben decided that the Mystery of the Vanishing Shoes was the weirdest. It had got worse too. All day long Ben had noticed more and more boys, girls and teachers sliding around the school in their socks.

It did explain the CURIOUS CASE of the INVISIBLE CHEESE, though. It wasn't cheese at all. It was Tabitha Fudge. Her shoes had vanished too, and she had the kind of socks that ponged of mouldy old Cheddar so badly that they ought to have been removed to a safe distance and destroyed in a controlled explosion!

The last lesson of the day was soon over, and Ben was on his way to fetch his coat for the chilly walk home. He was deep in thought. If only he could solve *The Mystery of the Vanishing Shoes*, then . . .

Watch out, Pole!

A small boy with a snotty
nose came skidding round the corner in his
socks and almost knocked Ben clean off his feet.

'It's STENCH!' he shouted, as he ran past and
sped off down the corridor. 'Run for it!'

Before Ben had a chance to change
course he bumped straight
into six feet of starched
white nylon.

BONK!

'NURSE STENCH!' he blurted. 'Er, I mean Tench. Nurse Tench . . .' His voice faltered as he looked up into the cold eyes of the school nurse. 'Um, hello?'

There was never a good time to bump into Nurse Tench. She was old, mad as a haddock, and the only thing she liked less than children was germs. She was crazy about them! She had a nasty habit of patrolling the hallways on the lookout for signs of contamination. Any hapless kid found with a runny nose or a sniffle would either be spritzed full in the face with her anti-bacterial spray, or dusted willy-nilly with noxious powders. Children and teachers ran and hid whenever they heard her battle cry echoing along the corridors.

'PUT a STOP to SNOTS and GROTS!'

So, bumping into Tench in the summer was bad enough, but now it was WINTER! And FLU SEASON! Disaster!

41

Tench glowered at Ben. She had a particularly wild look about her, so Ben shut his eyes and braced himself for the inevitable spritzing.

But nothing happened. He opened his eyes cautiously.

'Shoes!' barked Tench, holding out her gloved hand expectantly.

'Huh?' said Ben, thoroughly bamboozled. 'Um, what?'

'Your shoes, Pole,' said Tench, leaning close enough for Ben to get a whiff of the disinfectant Tench dabbed behind her ears instead of perfume. Pine-scented.

'For decontamination,' she said, snapping her fingers impatiently. 'Snots and grots, Pole, snots and grots!'

Ben slipped off his shoes and handed them over.

Tench snatched them up, spun on her heel and strode off down the corridor in pursuit of her next victim, the creak of her knees echoing along the hallway.

You there! Tommy Spangles! Shoes!

43

Ben let out a long breath and slumped against the wall. Well, he thought, at least I know where all the shoes are going.

But there were more questions to be answered. Like, what was Tench up to?

'And more importantly' – he looked at his feet and wiggled his toes –

How am I going to get home without frosbite?

CHAPTER THREE

The Poles' kitchen was warm and cosy, and something delicious bubbled in a pan on the stove.

The back door banged open and Ben clumped in through a flurry of snowflakes.

Hi, Mum!
Hi, Dad!

'Hello, love,' said Mrs Pole, helping Ben off with his coat. 'What on *earth* are you wearing?'

Ben huffed on his chilly fingers and sat down at the table. 'Well, *that* is an old cornflakes box,' he said, pointing at one foot, 'and *that's* half a coconut shell,' he added, waggling the other.

'Let me guess,' said Mr Pole, who was at the sink filling the kettle. 'Tench has gone off her rocker again?'

'Who's gone off her rocker?' asked a familiar voice from above.

Cornflakes box

Coconut shell

Ben and his mum and dad looked up. The Gasbag Glider was moored to the chimney and Coo and Herbert were perched on the edge of the skylight in the kitchen ceiling.

'Ah, Coo! You made it! Marvellous!' Mr Pole beamed as Coo and Herbert hopped down through the window.

'It's Tench again!' said Ben, nodding a hello at Coo and giving Herbert a welcoming scratch behind his ears. 'Today she confiscated my shoes for *decontamination*! She's gone crackers!'

'Crazy in the coconut,' agreed Coo, shaking snow from her crown and propping her spear against the wall. She turned and aimed a wide smile at Mr Pole. 'So, Mr P. Ben said you wanted to see me?'

'Ah, yes, Coo! I do! I have a surprise!' said Mr Pole, rubbing his hands together. 'Come with me. We'll nip out while the tea's brewing. It's in my shed. This way.'

Coo raised an eyebrow at Ben.

'Don't ask me.' Ben shrugged as they followed Mr Pole out into the garden. 'He's been banging about in there for weeks.'

So, no beard today then?

Well, you know how it confuses people...

'Did you know Tench was the school nurse when I was a boy?' Mr Pole chuckled. 'Tench the Terrible, we called her. My pal Sid went missing for three days one time. Turned out Tench had locked him up in an isolation pod in her office! Ha! Poor Sid only had the hiccups! Sounds like Tench is still as mad as a badger. A-ha! Here we are!' he announced as they reached the shed. He grabbed the door handle. 'Ready?'

The shed was full to bursting with weird and wonderful machines that creaked, clanked, hissed and burbled all around them.

'You HAVE been busy, Mr P.'

'Ha! I KNEW you'd love 'em, Coo! It was you who gave me the idea, actually,' said Mr Pole, clapping her on the back.

'What . . . *are* they?' wondered Ben.

'My inventions!' said Mr Pole. 'My contraptions! Don't be shy, have a look around!'

Ben and Coo moved from one machine to the next, pulling levers, twisting knobs and pressing buttons.

They flinched and ducked as the contraptions sparked, whirled about or spurted jets of hot oil in every direction. Mr Pole looked on eagerly with a big smile on his face and explained what each contraption was for.

'Ha! Well, I think they're brilliant, Mr P. They're slightly deadly and enormously unpredictable, but I never let that stop *me*. Eh, Ben?' said Coo, nudging Ben in the ribs.

'Thanks, Coo!' Mr Pole beamed with pride. 'Help yourself anytime, y'know, if you fancy a spot of Mud 'n' Acorn marmalade or have a chicken that needs a polish.' He glanced at his watch. 'Ooh! I reckon the tea will be ready by now. Let's go in, shall we? Oh, Coo?' he added as they turned to leave. 'There's a fresh packet of Double Choc Crumblies in the garage, if you wouldn't mind?'

'Sure thing, Mr P. Leave it to me,' said Coo. 'Back in a tick.'

As soon as she was gone, Mr Pole started giggling and jiggling from one foot to the other, like a man with his trousers full of grasshoppers.

'What's up with you?' Ben frowned. 'You haven't been sampling your Gumboot Glory, have you?'

'Oh, just a little surprise for Coo.' said Mr Pole, winking at Ben and tapping the side of his nose. 'The CUSTARD-IZER!'

'The what?'

'The CUSTARD-IZER!' he whispered. 'My burglar trap contraption! I set it up in the garage. Who better to test it on than Coo, the king of contraptions? She'll love it!' He stepped over to the door and opened it a crack to peek out. 'Any moment now, there will be a PING, a POP, a SPLOOSH and a shriek! Just you wait!'

Ben held Herb and waited. And waited.

And waited some more.

Nothing.

'I don't understand,' said Ben's dad, opening the door and stepping out.

Wait here, lad, I'll go and see.

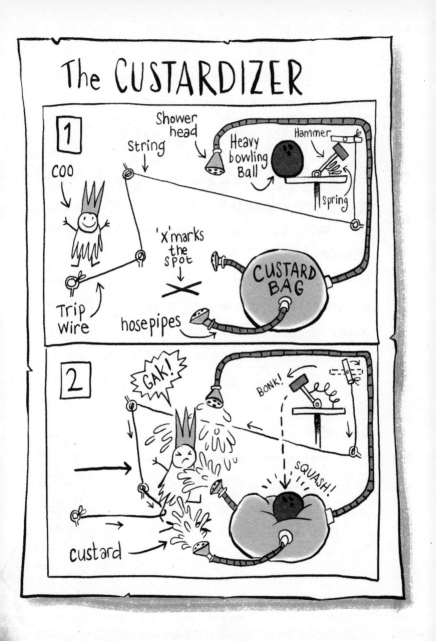

Ben was just thinking that Coo was the least likely person to fall for a trap when . . .

Ping! POP!
SPLOOSH! AAARGH!

'Dad?' called out Ben, trotting over to the garage. 'Coo?'

'Well, it works!' Mr Pole grinned. He was sitting on the floor and covered from top to toe in thick yellow gunge. Herb hopped onto his chest and licked his face, his rump wagging with pleasure.

'The quick-setting custard is a magnificent touch, Mr P,' said Coo, who was nonchalantly leaning against the garage wall nibbling a chocolate biscuit. 'And the second decoy tripwire almost caught me out. A bit more work and it'll be a cracker!' She pulled a camera from her bag and snapped a picture. 'One for the album, I reckon.'

'Oh, love, look at the state of you, you big lump,' chuckled Mrs Pole from the garage door. 'I was wondering what all that racket was! I might have guessed. Ben, Coo, hose him down, will you? And then you can all come in for your tea. Oh, and Ben?' she added, glancing at his feet. 'Get your shoes back tomorrow, won't you?'

'Sure thing, Mum.' Ben grinned.

'And don't worry, lad,' said Mr Pole, wiping custard from his beard. 'In the meantime, you can borrow a pair of mine. You'll love 'em. They're snazzy!'

Coo looked at Ben and winked.

CHAPTER FOUR

Ben's walk to school was a disaster! His dad's PARTY SHOES were at least a million sizes too big and Ben couldn't walk three steps without falling flat on his face in the snow.

MR POLE'S *PARTY* shoes

Tassles

GOLD TOECAPS

HUGE! Good to sit in and paddle across a <u>RIVER</u>, but deadly to walk in!

3 inch heels

fancy stitching

He paused at the school gates and rubbed his sore knees. Even wedging his sandwiches down the sides hadn't helped. The shoes were still deadly and now his lunch was mushed to a sticky paste. Ben sighed. He HAD to get his shoes back.

He walked gingerly up to the big school doors, took a deep breath, and went in.

'WATCH OUT THERE! NO BRAKES!' shrieked Miss Boon, the school librarian, as she whizzed past on a pair of roller skates.

Ben looked up and down the hallway. He couldn't believe it! Not a single person had escaped Tench's decontamination. There wasn't a school shoe in sight.

He clomped into assembly, sat next to Mandy Figgis who squeaked gently in an enormous pair of green waders, and planned to raid Tench's office the first chance he got. It was simple.

But as it turned out, getting past Tench wasn't as easy as he'd thought. Every time he tried to slip away, the barmy old fruit bat was always there! Either busily spraying things with powerful disinfectant, or putting up terrifying posters about the dangers of germs, or

dousing any passing kids with anti-nit powder.

There was no way his plan would work with her around. Her beady black eyes were always on the lookout and she'd be sure to spot him.

Ben needed a new plan, a Plan 'B'. And there was no time to lose. It was already his last lesson of the day.

He sat down and was furiously plotting what to do next, when he noticed a folded note on his desk.

After class Ben grabbed his bag and hurried to the headmaster's office. It was at the end of a long dim corridor and he was halfway there when – CLICK – everything went dark.

Ben lost his balance and skidded. 'WHOA!' His feet shot out from under him. 'AARGH!' And he landed in a heap. 'OOOF!' His bag spilled open across the floor.

'What the heck?' Ben lay panting in the dark, trying to catch his breath, when – CLICK – the lights came back on.

'Pole?' Mr Gigglethwick looked down at Ben. 'What on earth are you doing, boy?'

'You – you – you sent for me, Mr Gigglethwick,' said Ben breathlessly.

I did no such thing!

The headmaster frowned, clearly unimpressed.

'But—' said Ben.

'No buts, Pole!' interrupted the headmaster impatiently. 'I've told you before, stop mucking about! Now get along with you, it's time you went home! And clear up that mess!' he added, as he turned and tottered back into his office in a pair of Mrs Gigglethwick's red high-heeled boots.

Ben was just gathering up his things and stuffing them back into his bag, when the bell rang for home time.

The day was over.

It was time for *Plan B*.

There was a flurry of chatter and stamping feet as everyone piled out of the school and set off home through the snow. The noise faded into the distance until the only sound to be heard was the gentle whoosh of the wind outside.

Ben emerged from the lost property box at the far end of the main hall. He peeled an old football sock from his face and looked this way and that. It was all clear. Even Tench was nowhere to be seen!

He kicked off his gigantic shoes, hung them by their laces around his neck, and tiptoed up to the top floor and Tench's office.

Ben reached for the handle when a noise made him freeze. Someone was coming! Ben sprang back. He looked desperately up and down the corridor but it was long and empty.

There was nowhere to hide!

CHAPTER FIVE

Tench burst from her office. 'Who's that? Is someone there?'

Ben didn't dare move an inch. He held his breath and cocked an ear to listen.

71

'No time for nonsense! Got to go!' muttered Tench in a shrill, excited voice that sent a shiver up Ben's spine. 'Imagining it, was I? Crazy in the noggin, am I? Ha! I'll show *them*! They'll listen to me *now*!' She locked her door and hurried away down the corridor, pausing just long enough to slam the window shut – WHAM!

It was official. Ben was in a pickle.

He looked around for a way back inside.

Along the wall he could see the window to Tench's office. That one was wide open, but it was too far to reach. He could shout for help but that would do no good. The place was deserted. And he couldn't wait until the morning. He would be a frozen Ben-flavoured popsicle before midnight!

He shivered. If only Coo was here, he thought, *she'd* know what to do.

'Hold on! That's it!' he said, clicking his fingers.

The thingumajig!

Hugging the wall as best he could, Ben inched his bag from his shoulders. He opened it carefully and rummaged inside until he found what he was looking for.

He wasn't sure exactly what it was, but Coo had given it to him.

It was worth a try. Ben put the thing to his lips and blew.

THHPLLURRRT!

Nothing happened. Not a sausage. He blew it again. THHPLLURRRT!

Still nothing. He tried once more, but apart from getting dribble down his scarf, absolutely nothing happened.

'Oh, great,' said Ben grimly, hugging his knees to keep warm. 'Looks like it's popsicle time!'

He was just
wondering if he
could tie his clothes
together to make a rope when—

'POLE!'

Ben jumped and almost fell off his ledge.

'POLE!' The voice was coming from above.

'COO? Is that you?'

'Of course it's me! You blew Herbert's Hooter, didn't you?'

Ben looked up and saw the Gasbag Glider anchored to the school roof, and Coo and Herb leaning out over the edge above him.

'Herb's Hooter?'

'Yeah, it's like a dog whistle, but for wombats,' explained Coo, as though it was the most obvious thing in the world. 'He can hear it for miles. Sends him crackers! Doesn't it, fella?' She ruffled his chin affectionately.

'So, what's up? Isn't it a bit chilly to be mucking about on a ledge?'

'I'll explain in a minute!' said Ben, grinning like an idiot. He had never been happier to see his hairy friend. He pointed to the office window. 'I need to get in there.'

'Righto!' said Coo, vanishing from sight. 'Hold on!'

A moment or two passed by and Ben was just starting to wonder what was going on when Herbert appeared at the edge of the roof and stepped over.

Ben winced, expecting him to tumble down to the ground below, but he didn't.

SMUCK smuck.

Herb took a step towards Ben.

SMUCK smuck SMUCK smuck SMUCK smuck.

Like a tubby hairy gecko, Herbert waddled down the sheer wall to Ben, a suction cup on each of his four paws and a saddle around his waist.

'CLIMB ABOARD!' yelled Coo from above.

'WHAT?'

'GET ON! It'll be fine!' said Coo. 'Herb will carry you to the window.'

'You make it sound so simple,' said Ben, as he reached out with trembling hands and grabbed hold of Herb's saddle.

'So long as you don't let go,' added Coo quietly.

'Oh, NOW YOU TELL ME!' said Ben, swinging his legs around Herb's belly and clinging on for dear life.

Herb didn't seem bothered by the height and casually *smucked* his way to the open window. Ben clambered through, landing in a heap on the office floor.

'That's the way, Pole! You're a natural!' Coo chuckled as she swung through the window on the end of a rope, somersaulted and landed perfectly beside Ben.

Ben got to his feet and quickly explained what had happened.

'All that for a pair of *shoes!*' Coo shook her head and grinned as she and Ben began exploring the office.

'Well, yeah,' said Ben sheepishly. 'I know. But there's more to it, I'm sure of it. Tench has been *especially* odd lately!' Glass cabinets and medicine chests lined the walls, brimming with packets of tablets, bottles of foul-looking treatments and all manner of bandages, syringes and equipment. But there was no sign of his shoes.

'Hold on, what's this?' said Coo, spotting a door behind Tench's desk. She pushed it open and stepped through.

'There's definitely *something* strange going on,' said Ben, following Coo into the back room as she flicked on the light switch.

Coo whistled. 'You weren't kidding when you said Tench was crackers!'

Ben's skin tingled with goose bumps as he looked around the room. In the middle of a little desk was a notebook with TOP SECRET written across it in big letters. Ben picked it up gingerly, flicked through the pages to the final entry and gasped.

CHAPTER SIX

'Wow!' said Coo, leaning in to look over Ben's shoulder. 'This *is* weird! Is it *all* like this? Go back a bit.'

Ben's hands trembled slightly as he flicked back to the beginning and started to read the pages out loud.

Daily report

I caught Oscar Pilkington <u>SNEEZING</u> outside the maths room.

SYMPTOMS:
- damp handkerchief
- clammy brow
- watery eyes

DIAGNOSIS:
- contamination risk = 84%

Treatment:
- sprayed with <u>MAX</u> dose of SNOT-B-GONE 714X, plus one night in isolation pod

<u>Note</u>: order an extra tub of SNEEZE-AWAY powder, 3 onions and a tube of Wart cream.

'The first few pages look fairly normal to me,' said Ben. 'Well, normal for *Tench*, I mean.'

He skipped a few pages forward.

'Hold on!' said Coo. 'What was that? There!'

'Whoa!' Ben gasped. 'Now this *isn't* normal . . .'

'The Men in Caps?' said Ben. 'Who are they?'

'I'll tell you later,' said Coo. 'Go on. What else does she say?'

They **DON'T BELIEVE ME!**
They say they need <u>PROOF!!</u>
They won't listen!
They won't help. It's up to <u>ME</u>!
I must think of something...

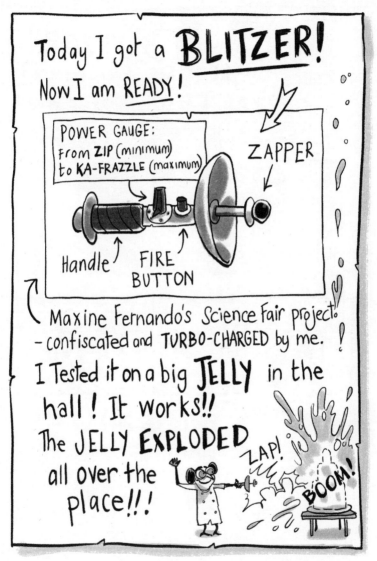

87

I'm glad I have my **BLITZER!**
There are **ALIENS** everywhere!!
But I **ZAPPED** them good and proper.

ALIEN 1
name: The Terror of TITAN
place: farmer's market

ALIEN 2
name: The BLOB monster from MARS
place: The children's Library

ALIEN 3
name: The mini-MENACE of MERCURY
place: The High Street

BUT the **MIC** still don't believe me!! I MUST find **PROOF!** I will start patrolling EVERY NIGHT!

'Well, *that* explains why it was raining jelly in assembly!' said Ben, turning the page. 'Crumbs! Look! Here's where I appear!'

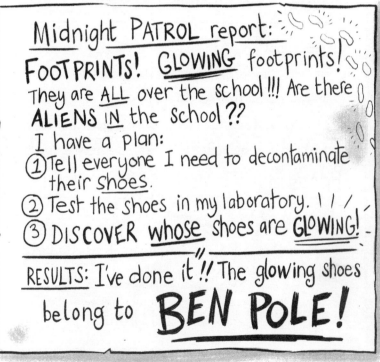

Midnight PATROL report:
FOOTPRINTS! GLOWING footprints!
They are ALL over the school !!! Are there
ALIENS IN the school ??
I have a plan:
① Tell everyone I need to decontaminate
   their shoes.
② Test the shoes in my laboratory.
③ DISCOVER whose shoes are GLOWING!
RESULTS: I've done it"!! The glowing shoes
belong to **BEN POLE!**

I always thought there was something SHIFTY about that boy, POLE! I will spy on him, but I mustn't let him find out I have discovered his SECRET until I know more. I must not scare him off.

Shifty Pole ⟵

'So that's why she pinched your shoes,' said Coo. 'I keep telling you to be more careful with the Glowshroom juice!' she added. 'It's strong stuff.'

'It was Herb's fault,' protested Ben. 'You know how over-excited he gets.'

Coo raised an eyebrow and read on. 'Hey, look here! It looks like Tench has a knack for traps.'

'Let's see,' said Ben.

'Ha! Not bad. A bit crude, but not bad!' said Coo.

Ben nudged her in the ribs. 'Oi! Whose side are you on? That hurt, that did! And now Mr Gigglethwick thinks I'm an idiot too! AND how dare she search my private stuff! Oh, hang on!' said Ben, frowning. 'This doesn't look good . . .'

Ben stopped reading. He had a bad feeling. He peered at the photo. 'I don't understand. It's just that selfie of me and Herb I took in your woods with your COO-mera.'

'Hold on!' said Coo. 'What's that in the background?'

'Dunno,' said Ben, squinting. 'I can't make it out.'

Coo rummaged through the desk drawer and found a large magnifying glass.

'Here, try this,' she said.

Ben had a much closer look. There, blurred but definitely visible, was something strange. It was tall and hairy, with long arms and legs and in the middle of its round body was a single massive eye!

Ben gasped.

'Uh-oh!' he said, turning to Coo.

CHAPTER SEVEN

The two agents looked up as urgent footsteps click-clacked across the polished stone floor of the lobby of the MIC headquarters.

'Uh-oh, look out, Fumble!' muttered the tall one under his breath, stiffening in his seat.

'Ugh! She's not back again, is she? How many times is that now?'

'I tell you, if I ever get my hands on the goon who leaked our address on the internet, I'll flippin' well— Ah, Ms Tench! What can we do for you today? You'll be wanting to see the Commander again, I suppose?'

'That's right, I do,' said Nurse Tench. 'And be quick about it!'

'She won't see you,' said Burke. 'Not after the last few times. All those *aliens* you spotted?'

'What *exactly* do you mean by that?' Tench glowered.

'Well, let me see,' said Burke, counting on his fingers. 'First of all, there was the dreaded Terror of Titan at the farmers' market.'

'Yes?'

'It wasn't an alien after all, was it?'

'It was an easy mistake to make.'

'It was a turnip, wasn't it?'

Fumble sniggered.

'Well, yes.' Tench clenched her jaw. 'But it was a big one. And organic.'

'Then there was the Blob Monster from Mars in the children's library,' continued Burke.

'It *looked* alien,' grumbled Tench.

'*All* beanbags look like that, Ms Tench.' Fumble chuckled, leaning back in his chair with a silly grin on his face.

'And just the other day,' said Burke. 'The Mini-Menace of Mercury in the high street? It was a miniature poodle, wasn't it? The *Commander's* miniature poodle.'

'Now, *that* did look weird!' protested Tench.

'Of *course* it did! It had just been *groomed*, Nurse Tench. The Commander was furious.'

'If only you hadn't Blitzed first and then asked questions afterwards, it might not have been so bad,' said Fumble. 'Perhaps you should just stick to your day job and leave the *alien* stuff to us, eh?'

The two agents grinned at each other and rolled their eyes.

'Don't think I don't remember you from your school days, Colin Fumble,' said Tench, leaning forward menacingly. Her left eyelid flickered. 'Still burp, do you, when you're nervous?'

The agents fell silent. Tench curled her lip. 'Or you, Leslie Burke. Spuds still bring you out in spots, do they? You two might be MIC agents now, but watch it. You're not too old for a spritzing.'

Tench glared at the two agents unblinkingly for a long moment.

Fumble burped.

Tench grinned and grabbed something from her bag then slammed it onto the desk.

'The Commander will see me THIS TIME!' she said. 'There IS an ALIEN! I have PROOF!'

Burke looked down at the desk, and then back up at Tench. He turned to Fumble and jerked his head towards the doors behind them. Without a word, Fumble pressed some numbers on the code pad and disappeared inside.

BEEP!
BEEP!
BEEP!

A moment later, the doors pinged and hissed open again.

'So, you're back, are you?'

The Commander was about as wide as she was tall. She had curly hair, a small mouth and a steely gaze. She was dressed in the same black suit and cap as the other agents, but her cap was the biggest of all.

'This had better be good, Ms Tench. I'm a busy woman,' said the Commander through gritted

teeth. 'Where's this *proof*, then?'

'Right here,' said Tench, holding out the photo she had nabbed from Ben's bag. 'There! An ALIEN – beside that boy, Ben Pole.' Tench's eyes glittered.

'That's not an *alien*, Ms Tench.' The Commander sighed and rolled her eyes impatiently. 'That's a *wombat!*' She turned to leave.

'NO!' yelled Tench triumphantly. '*Behind* the wombat!'

The Commander leaned in close for a second look.

'Well, well, well,' said the Commander, slowly raising an eyebrow. She straightened. 'OK, Ms Tench. Tell us everything.'

CHAPTER EIGHT

The flight from the school back to Coo's woods hadn't taken long, but there was a chilly wind and Ben was looking forward to curling up in front of a blazing fire.

'They'll be coming after you next,' said Coo, snapping Ben out of his daydream.

They climbed out of the Gasbag Glider onto a jetty built high up in the branches of a tree that creaked and swayed in the wind.

'Who will?'

'The MIC. The Men in Caps, that's who,' said

Coo, as she hopped onto a steep slide that was lashed to the side of the jetty and whooshed out of sight.

'But who are the MIC?' asked Ben as he jumped in after her. His stomach lurched as he zoomed down through the trees, the cold air stinging his face, until at last the slide levelled out and funnelled Ben into a tube that corkscrewed down and around and around and down and spat him out into Coo's tree house. He dropped PLUMPF! into an enormous wombat-hair beanbag and lay there panting.

'They're a secret agency,' continued Coo calmly, without the slightest sign that *she'd* just been zooming along at a hundred miles per hour. 'They investigate any reports of aliens and UFOs and things like that.'

Ben rose up onto his elbows and brushed his hair out of his eyes. 'Really? But—'

WHAM!

Everything went dark as he was squashed deep into the beanbag. Herbert had followed them down the slide.

'Mmmmmmf!' mumbled Ben from under Herb's furry rump.

Coo reached in and helped Ben clamber breathlessly out of the beanbag.

She poked the fire into life with her spear and sat Ben beside it while she fetched him a mug of hot spiced ginger beer.

'So, why do you think they're after me?' asked Ben anxiously.

'Well, they've got that photo now, haven't they? They know *what* they are looking for, but they don't know *where* to look. Except they know *you* do,' said Coo. She plucked a couple of huge hot chestnuts from the Toasty Roaster and tossed one to Ben.

chimney

TOASTY ROASTER

① HOT air rises and turns fan

② Fan turns the cogs

③ Nuts pass over the fire

④ mmmm! Lovely Roasted nuts!

'You're the missing link.'

Ben nibbled his nut thoughtfully. 'How come you know so much about them?'

The firelight flickered across Coo's face. 'Have I not told you about the time I spent in Switzerland in the laboratory of the insanely famous and famously insane astronomer, astronaut and mad scientist Professor Heinrich Von Himmelsaffe?'

'No,' said Ben, who had long since stopped being surprised by Coo's stories of her life.

'Well, we crossed paths with the MIC more than once,' said Coo with a wink, as infuriatingly mysterious as ever.

'Are they dangerous?'

'They're *determined*,' said Coo, suddenly very serious. 'They are like a dog with a sausage. They won't let go. The only thing they want more than an alien is a UFO – and all the powerful technology its secrets will give them. If they think there's one here, they won't stop searching until they find it.

'Oh!' Ben gulped. The thought of Coo's wonderful ancient woods being torn down filled him with dread and sadness. This was Coo's home, and Herbert's too.

'Finish your drink and come with me!' said Coo, leaping to her feet and grabbing a harness from a peg by the door.

'Oh no! That's not for me again, is it?'

Coo turned and winked. 'Not this time!'

Just a few moments later, Ben found himself clinging to a little sled, pulled along by Herbert who bounded through the deep snow like a short tubby reindeer.

'Mush, Herbert! Mush!' shouted Coo as the sled shot through the forest.

'Doesn't he mind?' said Ben through a mouthful of hair, his face bumping against Coo's back.

'Oh, Herb loves it! Look how excited he is!' said Coo, gripping the reins as Herbert jumped across a narrow ravine, landing with a thump on the far side, his rump wagging like mad.

Ben gripped on tighter. 'Where are we going anyway?' he shouted over the wind.

'We need to find out if the Men in Caps believed what Tench told them,' said Coo. 'If we're lucky, they'll still just think she's barmy and ignore her.'

'And if they believe her?'

'Then this whole forest is in danger,' said Coo grimly, 'and so are you.'

The sled swerved between two enormous black boulders, skidded across a frozen pond and then stopped at the foot of a tree so tall Ben couldn't see its top branches.

'So how do we find out if the MIC believed Tench or not?' he said, hopping off the sled after Coo. She patted Herbert, dropped a pile of wombat treats at his feet and turned to Ben.

'I'll show you. It's this way.'

Ben followed her as she rummaged amongst some ivy and pulled a rope from its hiding place.

'Hold on tight, Pole!' she said. 'Going up!'

Coo yanked the rope, there was a loud BOING, and suddenly the ground fell away as she and Ben shot up through the branches.

'Blimey! That snaps you awake!' said Ben, climbing out of the landing net at the top of the tree.

'And it's quicker than the stairs!' chuckled Coo. 'Come on, we've got work to do.'

Ben gingerly stepped onto the narrow platform beside Coo. He looked around and gasped. They were at the tip-top of the tallest tree in the wood, with a view of the forest and the city beyond stretching out in every direction.

In the middle of the platform was a large and elaborate telescope.

'This,' said Coo proudly, 'is the SKY-HIGH-SPY-EYE!'

'The SIGH-SKY-EYE-PIE?'

'Ha-ha! No, Ben. It's the $S K Y - H I G H - S P Y - E Y E$!' Coo repeated slowly.

She climbed into the seat, and as she pulled levers and turned wheels, the enormous telescope spun, tilted and focused on this and that, searching the horizon.

The SKY-HIGH -SPY-EYE

'What are you looking for?' asked Ben, trying not to think of the ground a *million* miles below him.

'There!' said Coo, fine-tuning the focus with gentle tweaks of a polished wooden handle. 'I thought so. Here, take a look.' She stepped down to make space for Ben.

Ben put his eye to the scope and there, far away and far below, he saw it.

'It's just a van.'

'It's not just a van, Ben. It's an *ice-cream* van,' corrected Coo.

'So?'

Coo raised an eyebrow. 'An *ice-cream* van? In the *winter*?'

'Men in Caps?' said Ben, suddenly feeling anxious again.

'Yup, I reckon so. They're on patrol.' She turned to Ben.

Looks like they believed Tench after all!

CHAPTER NINE

All the next day the snow fell heavily. At the mid-morning break it already reached Ben's ankles, and by lunchtime it was deep enough to comfortably bury a fat badger – a *tall* fat badger.

But Ben couldn't enjoy it. He was back at school and feeling rattled.

Go to school. Say nothing. Coo had told him, her eyes glinting that way they always did when she was planning something spectacular. *Just act normal,* she'd added, as Ben had waved goodbye the day before.

That was easier said than done. So long as he was at school he was safe. The MIC wouldn't grab him here. But Ben still felt jumpy. Every time he caught Tench watching him with those beady eyes of hers, it took all his nerve not to bolt for the door, run away and hide in a bush.

And she wasn't the only thing making him extra nervous. That dinner lady, Doris, and the caretaker, Morris, for instance . . .

Are they new? thought Ben suspiciously.

Still, he couldn't be sure. Not absolutely.

The last bell of the day finally rang, and Ben knew this was when he was in the greatest danger of being nabbed. He was nervously walking along the hallway, keeping a sharp lookout for trouble, when Harry Trundle, a small round boy with pink cheeks, slouched past.

'I mean, why bother parking *right outside* if he isn't even open?' he complained loudly to Betsy Cabbage, the girl beside him, waving his arms about in the air with exasperation. 'He was SO rude! I only wanted a Mint-Choc-Ripple!'

'You *did* keep hammering on the shutter, though,' Betsy remarked, 'didn't you?'

Harry shrugged. 'Well, I'm HUNGRY, aren't I? There was no need for all that bad language!'

Hang on a minute, thought Ben as the pair

disappeared from view around the corner. *Mint-Choc-Ripple? In WINTER?* He trotted along the corridor the way they had come, slowing down to a shuffle as he approached the entrance hall. He crept closer until he had a clear view through the glass of the big double-doors that led out to the car park in front of the school.

Sure enough, there it was.

'The ice-cream van!' he whispered.

Ben ducked back as Nurse Tench suddenly loomed out of the swirling snow and knocked on the door of the van. Ben peered from the shadows to see what she was up to.

'I TOLD you we're SHUT, you greedy little ratbag!' growled an angry voice from inside the van as the door banged open. 'Oh, it's you. You're late. Get in here.'

Ben gasped as a big man with a moustache, wearing a long black coat and a black cap, stepped out of the van and ushered Tench inside.

'Doris!' Ben gulped.

The man's dark glasses glinted in the fading light as he scanned the car park before ducking back into the van and slamming the door shut.

Ben slipped away quietly from his hiding place. There wasn't an ice lolly in sight in that van. It was packed from floor to ceiling with electronic equipment that bleeped and whirred, and screens that blinked and flashed with coloured lights. And sitting at the back, also dressed in black, was 'Morris'.

Coo was right! It *was* the Men in Caps!

Ben had seen enough. He had to get back to the forest, and fast!

CHAPTER TEN

Ben eased open the big front doors, just wide enough to sneak out without being seen.

Red light flickered eerily through the windows of the ice-cream van as Ben crept past. The murmur of voices and the crackle of radios drowned out the quiet squeak and crunch of the snow beneath Ben's feet as he snuck out through the school gates and away into the city.

It was snowing harder than ever as he ran through the maze of back streets and alleyways to the secret entrance to Coo's woods. The afternoon light was fading fast, and by the time he was wading through the knee-deep snow beneath the enormous old trees, it was almost dark.

He clutched his coat tightly to his body and, shielding his eyes from the icy wind, Ben stared through the gloom, searching for any sign of Coo. He saw something shift up ahead and slip beneath a tree-lined ridge. Ben cupped his hands to his mouth to call out when—

'That's right, Pole.' She grinned, gripping him tightly in her bony grasp. Ben gasped as more figures emerged from the trees. Their black coats flapped in the wind and their caps were pulled down low over their eyes.

'W-w-what are *you* doing here?' stammered Ben.

'Thought you'd given us the slip, did you?' said Tench gleefully. 'Well, you're not as clever as you think, are you?' She turned Ben and pointed triumphantly at the ground behind him.

Ben stared, and there, clear as day, were his footprints in the snow. His *glowing* footprints, stretching all the way back from where he had come.

'B-but . . .' Ben gulped.

'You led us right where we wanted to go!' gloated Nurse Tench.

A short woman with a tall cap stepped forward and looked at Ben. 'Good work, Ms Tench,' she said in a low strong voice. 'Seems you're not entirely bonkers after all.'

'I told you, didn't I? I knew he'd lead us here eventually, Commander,' said Tench. 'This is *definitely* where that photo was taken.'

'Let me go!' protested Ben, wriggling to get free. But it was useless. No child had ever got free from Tench's iron-tight grip.

'Agent Burke! Agent Fumble!' barked the Commander. 'Keep an eye on the boy. The rest of you, spread out. Let's find this thing!'

Ben suddenly stopped wriggling and stared, his eyes wide as saucers. 'I wouldn't bother,' he said, pointing at the tree-lined ridge with a trembling finger. '

I think your THING has found us!

Everyone turned to look.

There, silhouetted against the faint light, stood the THING from SPACE!

It was tall, with long thin legs, and arms that reached the ground. In the middle of its round hairy body was a single massive eye that glowed with green flickering light.

'A-A-ALIEN!' screamed Tench, whipping a can of SUPER-STRONG-GROT-BE-GONE from her pocket and spraying herself from head to toe.

The Thing strode towards them through the trees on its spindly legs.

Ben stepped back as the agents snapped into action.

'ATTACK!' bellowed the Commander as the Thing came closer and closer.

Powerful torch beams lit up the Thing as the agents surrounded it, firing grappling hooks from all sides, and tangling its long legs in a web of ropes.

Ben watched as it twisted this way and that, struggling to get free, until at last it swayed and tottered and came crashing down, landing in the deep snow with an enormous WUMPF!

The Commander and her agents approached the Thing. Its huge eye flickered green, but it lay still.

'Let's get this back to base, men!' she ordered. 'Before we all freeze to death. And bring the boy too. I've got some questions for him!'

Walkie-talkies chattered and buzzed and a small tractor trundled into sight through the trees. Ben was bundled into the cab. Agents lashed the Thing

from Space to a trailer, and as soon as they were
ready, the tractor coughed to life and led Tench,
the Commander and her agents back out of Coo's
woods to their waiting vans and onward to MIC
headquarters.

Ben peered anxiously through the tractor's
window as they left and hoped that Coo was OK,
but all he could see was snow.

Chapter Eleven

The tractor parked in the enormous underground garage of the MIC headquarters and guards closed the huge gates behind them with a loud CLANG!

'We're here,' said Agent Burke, opening the cab door. 'Come with me. The Commander wants a word with you.'

Ben stepped nervously from the tractor and followed Burke while other agents locked up the Thing from Space in a giant cage with big thick steel bars.

'That *THING* must be destroyed!' said Tench, slamming her fists on the table. 'Did you see that hair! It must be teeming with SPACE NITS the size of walnuts! Who knows what foul SNOTS and GROTS it will infect us with!' Her eyelid twitched madly at the thought of it and she quickly sprayed herself again, full in the face, with her SUPER-STRONG-GROT-BE-GONE.

The Commander gritted her teeth. 'For the final time, Ms Tench, NO you may NOT blitz the ALIEN! And if you interrupt me again you will be asked to leave!'

Ben sat opposite them in the small and plain interview room. He was wrapped in a blanket and was warming his chilly hands around a mug of hot chocolate. He took a long slow slurp. He'd been given his first hot chocolate when the Commander had sat him down and had started asking him questions.

That was five mugs ago.

'OK, Mr Pole, let's start from the beginning again, shall we?' Her patience was clearly wearing thin. 'You agree that the woods where we found the alien are the same ones in the photo, yes?'

'Yup.'

'But you say you didn't know there was an *alien* in the woods until this afternoon?'

'If I had,' Ben paused to glug the rest of his drink, 'I would never have gone back in there, would I?'

'So, you've never seen the alien's UFO? The spaceship?' continued the Commander. 'You don't know where it is hidden?'

Ben put the empty mug on the table and licked his lips. 'Any chance of another hot chocolate?' he said, shivering. 'I'm still a tad chilly.'

'ENOUGH!' boomed the Commander, getting to her feet and towering over Ben. 'Just tell me, WHERE IS THE UFO?'

Ben looked up into her red face. 'How on earth would I know?' he said, shrugging his shoulders. 'I told you, I only go to the woods to feed the wombat. You haven't seen him, have you, by the way? He's about this big,' Ben said, holding his hand at Herbert-height above the ground. 'He's hairy, snuffly, and if I'm honest, a touch on the plump side. Oh, and he smells of cake.'

The Commander's face deepened from red to purple. 'I DON'T CARE ABOUT WOMBATS!' she shouted, waving her arms about in the air. 'I JUST HAVE TO FIND THAT UFO!'

Ben ran a finger around the inside of his mug. 'Look, it seems simple to me,' he said, licking chocolate from his fingertip. 'Why don't you just let the alien go free?'

Tench exploded. 'WHAAAT? You must be MAD!' she yelled, leaping to her feet and whipping out her Blitzer. It hummed into life, electric sparks crackling across its tip. 'That THING is going NOWHERE!'

'WAIT!' The Commander held up her hand. 'Hold on a minute! I think the boy might be on to something there.'

Burke and Fumble grabbed Tench by the arms and sat her back down.

'I mean, if I was the alien,' continued Ben calmly, 'and I got free from this place, the only thing I would want to do is go home, as quickly as I could. And to do that, I would need to go back to where I left my—'

'SPACESHIP!' said the Commander. 'Get this boy another hot chocolate, Fumble. He's earned it! Then, all of you, come with me! Let's get that THING out of here, and we'll see where it leads us!'

Chapter Twelve

The Thing from Space strode quickly along the deserted streets, barely making a sound, other than a strange creak and shuffle as it walked.

'It's working!' whispered the Commander. 'It's heading back to the woods.'

As soon as they had unlocked the cage and opened the gates, the Thing had risen awkwardly to its feet and headed out into the snowy night.

The Commander waved her hand, ordering Ben, Tench and the agents to follow her. 'Keep back so it doesn't spot us. And if it gives us the slip,' she added, turning to Ben and fixing him with a steely gaze, 'YOU have to help us find it!'

Ben said nothing as he stumbled through the snow, being dragged along by Tench. She had *demanded* to be there, as she was the one who had spotted the UFO in the first place.

They all crept quickly and carefully after the Thing.

Every now and then it would pause, turn its big eye up and down the street and then stride off in its chosen direction.

149

It was midnight by the time they reached the forest and the wind whistled eerily through the bare branches of the huge trees.

The alien's tracks led them deep into the woods and up over a rise in the ground where a faint green glow lit up the trees.

'What's that light?' said Burke.

'What's that bubbling sound?' said Fumble.

'What's that SMELL?' Tench gasped.

Ben knew where they were. He would recognize that whiff anywhere!

They crested the rise and there below them, bubbling and popping with puffs of foul gas, was the Hot Pong Bubble Swamp!

'Look!' said Tench. 'The mud's *glowing*! *That's* what Pole must've trodden in! *That's* what made his shoes glow!'

'Then this *must* be the place!' said the Commander. 'YES! There! Look!' She pointed, her wide eyes shining green in the eerie glow. 'The UFO!'

On the far side of the swamp, glowing bright green and hovering above the bubbling mud was the *weirdest*-looking thing Ben had ever seen!

It wasn't the sleek silver spacecraft they had all imagined. It was ugly, a jumble of strange machinery, a tangle of pipes and wires. Lights flickered and buzzed, pipes oozed and puffed smoke.

For a silent moment the group just stood there, rooted to the spot and gazing in wonder. The Commander couldn't believe her eyes! What fabulous secrets this UFO must hold!

And there, lit by the green glow, was the Thing from Space, gingerly skirting the swamp.

Suddenly the silence was shattered.

'IT'S BLITZING TIME!' screamed Tench, who had slipped away from the group, and with her Blitzer grasped in both hands, was taking aim at the Thing from Space.

'NOOOOO!' Ben cried, diving headlong at Tench and knocking her sideways. The Blitzer fired, sending a bolt of blue sparks crackling and sizzling into the swamp just centimetres from the alien's feet.

With an enormous KA-PLOOOOOMPF! a huge plume of stinking hot mud shot high into the air and came showering down, drenching Tench from head to foot in the glowing gloop!

The shot had missed, but it had done enough. The blast had knocked the gangly alien off balance, and now it teetered and tottered on the edge of the swamp.

'Tench! What have you done!' shouted the Commander.

Ben watched helplessly as the alien fell forwards. For a moment it slipped from view in the swirling gas and then splashed into the sucking swamp.

Everyone rushed forward, but the Thing from Space sank quickly and vanished below the surface. The glow of its green eye faded away beneath a final frothy burst of bubbles. It was lost in the swamp for ever.

'HA-HA-HA-HA!' Tench cackled, mud dripping from her nose. 'The SNOTS and GROTS are

GONE! The SNOTS and GROTS are gone for good!' She whooped, hopping from one foot to the other with horrible delight.

'Fumble!' ordered the Commander, pointing at Tench. 'Restrain that woman! And confiscate that BLITZER too! Burke, scan the swamp for danger!'

Bleep . . .

'The rest of you, prepare to grab the UFO!'

Bleep . . . bleep . . . bleep . . .

'Fetch the grappling hooks and radio for the tractor. We will need the trailer.'

Bleep.bleep.bleep.bleep.bleep.bleep.bleep . . .

'And Burke!' she yelled. 'What IS that noise?'

'It's our scanners, ma'am!' said Burke, holding up the electronic gizmo for her to see. 'They've gone NUTS!'

The little screen flashed with a red skull-and-crossbones and it was bleeping like crazy.

'Well, that doesn't look good! What is it? Is the alien *alive*?'

'No, ma'am! It's the swamp!' said Burke. 'It's contaminated. That glowing green alien goo! It's like nothing we've ever seen!'

'Here, let me check,' said the Commander. Grabbing the scanner, she turned to Tench and swept the gizmo over the green swamp mud that still covered her from top to toe.

BLEEPBLEEPBLEEPBLEEPBLEEP!

The scanner bleeped louder than ever.

'Wait! No, I can't be . . . c-c-contaminated!' Tench quivered, furiously brushing the mud from her sleeves and flicking it from her fingertips. 'No! Not me. Not with ALIEN GROTS!'

Ben leaned over for a closer look. 'Is it dangerous?'

Burke checked the readings. He looked at the Commander. His face was pale. 'Very extremely, utterly super-dangerous, ma'am! We've got to get OUT of here!'

'Wait! What?' said Tench.

'Agents!' boomed the Commander. 'This swamp is HIGHLY CONTAMINATED! Get that UFO back to base and into IMMEDIATE quarantine! And I want this whole area designated a NO-GO ZONE! It is DEADLY!' She turned to Tench. 'And Fumble, pop Ms Tench into a quarantine pod too.'

'No . . . not me . . .' Tench wailed as Fumble escorted her away. 'Not meeeee!'

There was a flurry of activity as the agents strapped the UFO onto the trailer of the tractor and carefully dragged it out of the woods and back to the safety and secrecy of the MIC headquarters.

With the UFO and the deadly alien goo to worry about, everyone had forgotten about Ben.

Amidst the swirling snow, the bustling agents, the bobbing flashlights and the crackle of radio chatter, he slipped away and hid until everyone had gone.

When he was finally alone he emerged, cold and tired, and ran to the edge of the Hot Pong Bubble Swamp. He fell to his knees and peered into the murky glowing mud for any sign of life.

There was nothing.

'Coo?' Ben said in a choked voice.

'All right, Pole?' said a voice behind him. 'Dropped something, have you?'

Ben spun round. 'COO! It's you! You're OK!'

'Never better!' She grinned, straightening her crown.

Chapter Thirteen

'I found a glob of custard behind my ear yesterday!' said Mr Pole proudly, putting a tray of tea and toasted crumpets on the little table in the sitting room. 'But I think that was the last of it.'

Morning sunlight flooded in through the windows. Ben and Coo had arrived just in time for breakfast.

'That's enough about your Custardizer, my love,' said Mrs Pole, patting a cushion beside her. 'Coo, sit by me and tell us what you two have been up to. How was your sleepover? Fun, was it?'

'Yes, thanks, Mrs P,' said Coo, dropping onto the sofa while Herb plonked himself in front of the fire, shuffling onto his back to warm his belly. She grabbed a buttery crumpet and took a huge bite. 'Ahh, that's better. I'm starving! I tell you, Mrs P, aliens are hard work.'

Mr Pole dropped his teacup. 'Wait! WHAT?'

'ALIENS?' Mrs Pole gasped.

'Yup!' Ben grinned. 'And I spent the night with secret agents of the MIC!'

Mr Pole dropped his crumpet. 'The MEN IN CAPS? The alien hunters? Wait, you mean they're *real*?'

Coo looked at Ben's mum and dad, sitting there with their mouths hung open in amazement, and smiled. 'It's OK. It's all over now. Perhaps we'd better start at the beginning.'

They settled back with cups of tea and listened as Ben and Coo explained.

'It was all because of that clumsy lump,' said Coo, nudging Herb with her toe. 'He knocked a keg of Glowshroom juice over Ben's shoes.'

'I've been leaving a trail of glowing footprints everywhere I go!' said Ben.

'Oh, I see!' said Mrs Pole. 'Is *that* why Nurse Tench confiscated your shoes?'

'Yeah, exactly,' said Ben. Between slurps of tea he explained about raiding Tench's office, what they had found in her diary and all about how she had spotted a UFO and become obsessed with aliens and intergalactic snots and grots. '*And* she found this in my bag, the crafty old prune!' he added, showing them the photo of him and Herb in the woods.

'Hold on! Is *THAT* an *ALIEN?*' said Mr Pole, pointing at the photo with a buttery finger. 'There! In the background, right behind you?'

'Oh my!' Mrs Pole gulped.

'Well, that's what the MIC thought,' said Coo, 'when Tench showed them the picture. But the funny thing is . . .' Coo raised an eyebrow. 'There never *was* an alien in the first place!'

'Huh?' Mr Pole stopped chewing.

'The Thing in the photo that Tench saw was just me, testing out my new Snow-Go!'

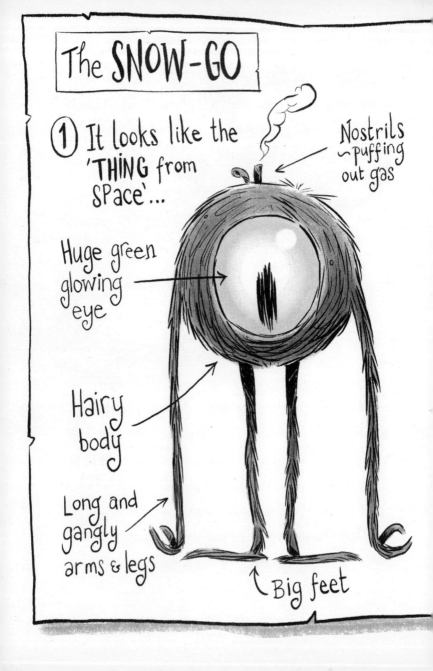

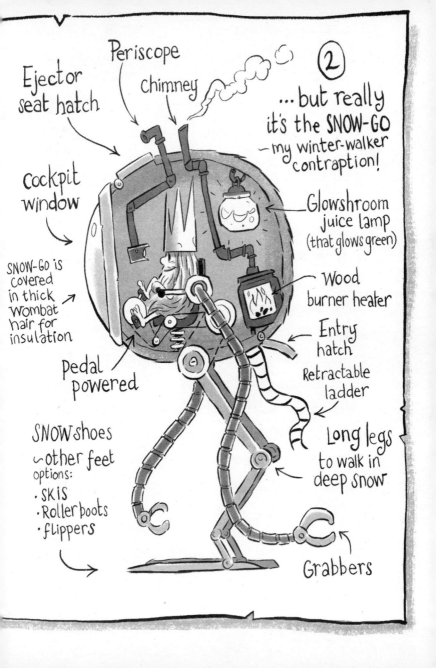

Ben sat forward in his armchair. 'We knew the MIC would tear down the woods searching for the alien and the UFO! There was no stopping them, even if we told them there wasn't an alien till we were blue in the face!'

'So, the plan was simple really,' said Coo, casually tossing Herb a crumpet. 'If they wanted an alien, we'd give them one!'

'And a UFO too.' Ben grinned.

'So *that's* why you wanted all Mr Pole's crazy gadgets!' Mrs Pole chuckled. 'Oh, how wonderful!'

'Yup! I bolted them all together, painted them with Glowshroom juice, and sprinkled them with enough Float Juice to make the whole thing hover!' said Coo. 'It worked a treat!'

'What do you mean . . . *crazy gadgets?*' Mr Pole sniffed. 'I thought you *liked* them. You told me a professor from the university had borrowed them for research. You said he'd called them "Inspirational".'

'Ah, yes. Sorry, love.' Mrs Pole patted his arm.

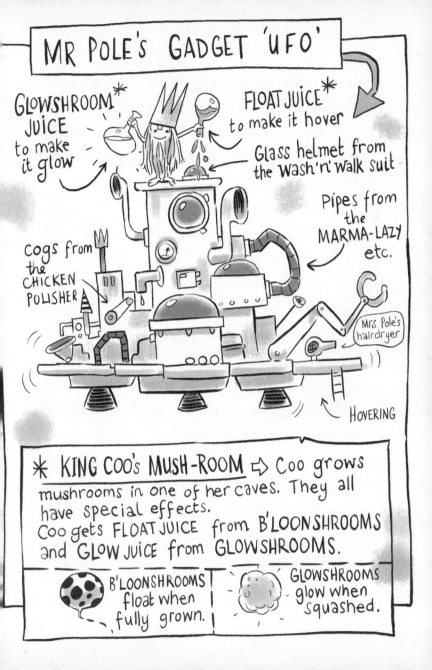

'But when Coo asked for them, I *knew* it would be for a good reason.'

Mr Pole shuffled his feet. 'Oh well, I *suppose* it's OK. Hey, not bad though, them being used to build a UFO!' he added brightly.

'So the "Alien" and the "UFO" were all ready for the MIC to "discover", said Coo. 'The tricky bit was figuring out how to make sure that when the MIC left with what they wanted, they'd NEVER come back!'

'I have a feeling' – Mr Pole smiled and rubbed his hands together – 'that you came up with a plan for that too!'

Coo grinned. 'First of all, I tipped my WHOLE supply of Glowshroom juice into the Hot Pong Bubble Swamp to make it glow green. Then I tinkered with the MIC's scanners to make them go CRAZY at the first whiff of the swamp mud, so they'd think the whole place was dangerously contaminated with deadly alien goo.'

'They made the whole place a no-go zone!' Ben chuckled. 'Not only will they never come back themselves, they are actually stopping ANYONE else from going into the woods either. Well, anyone who doesn't know the secret ways in, that is. It's perfect!'

'Hold on, Coo.' Mr Pole frowned. 'You know how to tinker with highly complex electronic scanners?'

'One day I'll tell you about my summer at the Boffin Academy in Kuala Lumpur building robots with the electronics genius Dr Wally Waffle-Burger.' Coo grinned.

'But they must keep those scanners in their headquarters or a secret base or something?' said Mrs Pole. 'And surely it would be teeming with guards? There would be no way in, would there?'

Coo licked butter from her fingers and smiled. 'Ah, that's my favourite bit. I got them to take us in there *themselves*! Look!'

She shoved the tea tray to one side and explained it all with pencil and paper.

So...

'You blinking genius!' said Mr Pole, slumping back into his chair. 'Amazing! You two have done it again!'

'Not bad, eh, Dad?' said Ben. 'The Thing from Space is gone. The MIC have the UFO they were looking for, and the "contaminated" green goo keeps the woods safe.'

'Ha! Wonderful!' said Mrs Pole, clapping her hands.

'The only dodgy moment was when Tench tried to blitz Coo before she had a chance to hop out and sink the Snow-Go,' said Ben. 'I thought you were going to get fried for sure!'

'That's what ejector seats are for, Pole, old pal!' Coo winked. 'Safety first!'

'Ha! SAFETY FIRST? YOU?' Ben grinned. 'Don't make me laugh!'

BOING!

'But if there was never really an alien,' said Mrs Pole. 'Then what was it that Nurse Tench spotted that night?'

'Ah! That was *you*, wasn't it, Herb?' said Coo, bending down to scratch Herb's belly. 'We were testing out my HIGH-FLY-FLOAT-SUIT,' she explained.

'Herb tripped and fell in the tub of Float Juice, the clumsy lump,' smiled Coo. 'Shot straight up

FLOAT-JUICE tank

Sprinklers

Remote control valve

Romper suit dipped in Glowshroom Juice *

* Glows in the dark for easy tracking at night

HERB'S HIGH-FLY-FLOAT-SUIT

through the roof, didn't you, fella? Thankfully he drifted back down eventually.'

'Ha! No wonder Tench thought she had spotted a UFO!' Mr Pole chuckled, handing round another plate of freshly toasted crumpets. 'Well, what a story! Fantastic! Um, Coo?' he added, with a twinkle in his eye. 'I don't suppose you have any of that Float Juice in your bag, do you?'

CHAPTER FOURTEEN

The snow crunched under Ben's feet as he followed Coo and Herbert through the woods. The trees sparkled with frost in the morning sunlight.

'Did your dad get down OK?' said Coo, hopping over a fallen log.

'Ha! Yes! Eventually.' Ben giggled. 'I don't know *what* he was thinking, sprinkling his slippers with that Float Juice of yours.'

Coo laughed. 'Yeah, strong stuff, that.'

'He was pressed up against the sitting-room ceiling for an hour and a half!' said Ben. 'We had to toss him sausage rolls and apples at lunchtime, but it wore off in the end and we managed to hook him down with a broom.'

It had been a few days since the night of the ALIEN and things were slowly getting back to normal. *Well, as normal as life with Coo can be,* Ben thought, glancing happily at her.

He tossed a snowball for Herb to chase. 'Oh, did you hear about Nurse Tench?'

'Still barmy, I suppose?' said Coo.

'Not so much actually,' said Ben. 'Apparently, since she's been stuck in the MIC's quarantine pod, she's happier than ever. She decided that it's the safest place for her. No SNOTS and GROTS are going to catch up with her in there!'

'Ha! Well, I'm happy for her, the mad old sprout.' Coo smiled. 'Ah, here we are.'

The Hot Pong Bubble Swamp steamed and burbled and popped puffs of olive-green gas into the crisp winter air.

'It looks cool,' said Ben, pinching his nose. 'But it still smells like a shoebox full of mouldy old socks!'

'More like the bus home from a meeting of the Cabbage-Tasters Club!' Coo snorted.

Ben looked at the deep swamp. 'It's a shame about your Snow-Go,' he said. 'That looked amazing, that did. And I never got to have a ride.'

'Oh, I wouldn't worry,' said Coo, fishing about in her beard. She took out a pocket-sized sundial and turned it on the palm of her hand. 'Let's see now. It's been . . . um . . . three days, four hours and . . . twenty-seven minutes, so . . .' she said, pulling out a little umbrella and popping it open with the click of a button. 'In five seconds . . . four . . . three . . . two . . .

Ben leaped for cover and peeked out from under Coo's umbrella as an ENORMOUS jet of swamp mud, froth and steam gushed up into the air.

Falling mud pitter-pattered all around, and then something big landed with a loud wet SPLAT.

Ben turned and peered through the fading steam.

The SNOW-GO!

'Regular as clockwork, that geyser.' Coo winked. 'Now come on, Pole, help me rinse it off and I'll take you for a spin.'

It didn't take them long to clean up the Snow-Go and Ben was soon being hauled into the cockpit by Coo.

It was a bit of a struggle squeezing in two kids and a fat wombat, but they managed it and were soon striding through the snowy forest with Coo at the controls and Ben and Herb gazing out through the big round window and grinning like idiots with the excitement of it all.

As the Snow-Go loped through the deep snow, Ben chuckled to himself. 'I've got to say, that was another cracking plan of yours.' He grinned. 'I mean, using Dad's gadgets to fake the UFO was a stroke of genius!'

'Thanks, Pole,' said Coo. 'Well, I wasn't going to let them take my UFO, was I?'

Ben's mouth dropped open. 'Huh?'

'My UFO,' said Coo. 'The one in the cave.'

'Wait. What?'

'See? There,' said Coo, pointing into the dark. They were standing on a ledge in a dark cave and below them, beside an underground pool of still water, was the UFO. A *real* UFO! Its sleek silver saucer glimmered in the faint light from Coo's firefly lantern. 'It's been here for years.'

'What? And you never thought to mention it?' spluttered Ben.

'You don't half make a fuss, Pole.' Coo laughed as she clambered down to the spaceship and climbed on board. She patted the seat beside her and Ben followed and got in.

'Does it work?' he asked, gazing at the single glowing button on the control panel.

'Dunno,' said Coo, closing the hatch. 'Let's see, shall we?'

'Really?'

'Yup!' said Coo.

Ben grinned,

and pressed the button.

CLICK!

ACKNOWLEDGEMENTS

I'd like to thank everyone at David Fickling Books for their boundless enthusiasm during the making of this book. Thank you Rosie, my fantastic editor, for your ever-cheerful guidance and encouragement, and Alison, my brilliant designer, for helping to bring this book together so beautifully.

I would also like to thank: Tamlyn and Caroline at Arena Illustration for their friendship and all their hard work on my behalf,

My wonderful family and friends for their support, and especially my wife Zoë, and my daughter, Mary, for their love and patience.

About Adam Stower

Author photo: Paul Winter

Adam Stower is an award-winning author and illustrator of children's books.

His books have received international acclaim, winning prizes at home and abroad, including The Alligators Mouth Award 2020 for *King Coo: The Curse of the Mummy's Gold*, the Red House Book Award for *Bottom's Up!* (Author – Jeanne Willis) 2010 and the Wanda Gag Read-Aloud Book Award (US) for *Silly Doggy!* 2013.

Much of *King Coo* was inspired by Adam's memories of playing in the woods with his brother, Matt, and of the time he spent at a 462-year-old boarding school in north Norfolk.

Adam lives in Brighton with his wife, his daughter and a cat called Murray.